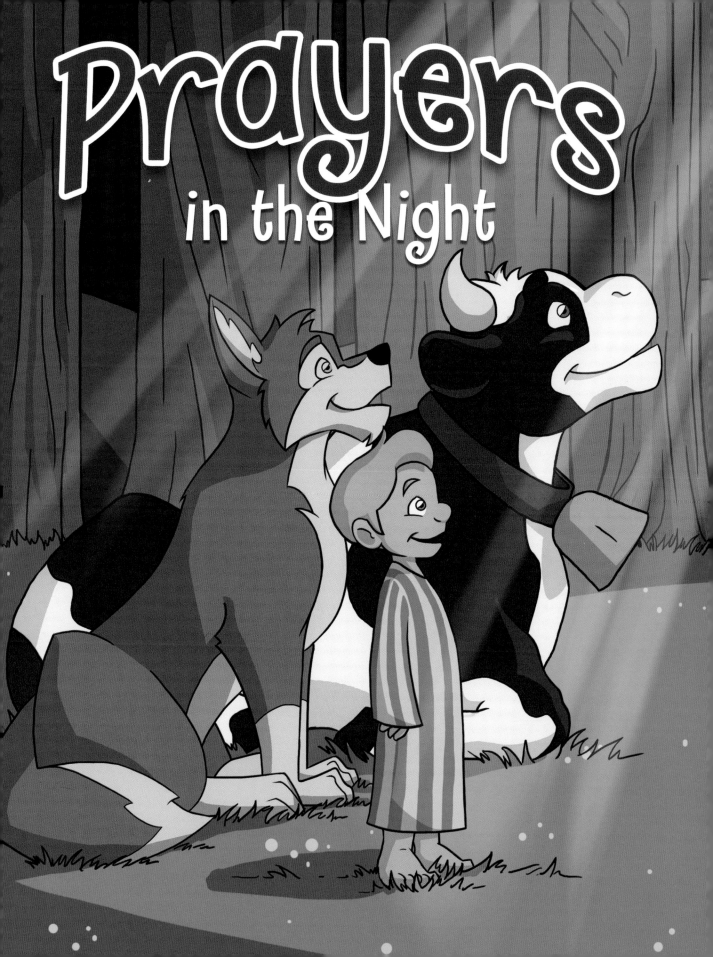

For Julie
and Hailey,
my guiding
stars

Text & Illustrations © 2018 Cason Smithson
All rights reserved.

This is not an official publication of The Church of Jesus Christ of Latter-day Saints. The opinions and views expressed herein belong solely to the author and do not necessarily represent the opinions or views of Cedar Fort, Inc. Permission for the use of sources, graphics, and photos is also solely the responsibility of the author.

ISBN 13: 978-1-4621-2271-4

Published by CFI, an imprint of Cedar Fort, Inc.
2373 W. 700 S., Springville, UT 84663
Distributed by Cedar Fort, Inc., www.cedarfort.com

Library of Congress Control Number: 2018946470

Cover design and typesetting by Shawnda T. Craig
Cover design © 2018 Cedar Fort, Inc.
Edited by Kaitlin Barwick

Printed in the United States of America

10 9 8 7 6 5 4 3 2 1

Printed on acid-free paper

Prayers
in the Night

Written and Illustrated by Cason Smithson
CFI • An imprint of Cedar Fort, Inc. • Springville, Utah

Deep in the forest,
where large oak trees stood,
warm light filled the air,
just as any light would.

A strong alpha wolf,
watching over his pack,
was first to feel fear
as the forest turned black.

He searched and he sniffed
for his mate and his pups,
but in the darkness he lost them
and was about to give up!

He sank in his sadness,
on the cold earth he lay.
Lost and alone, he decided to pray.

"Heavenly Father," he cried
to the night that was deep,
"I have become like a little lost sheep."

He turned to the sky,
where no stars
or moon stood,
and asked
Heavenly Father
to send light if He could.
He promised he'd wait
and believe all the while.
And as he sat and listened,
he started to smile.

He had not gone far, not as far as he thought.
And he saw in the light what before he could not.
His pups and his mate rested under a tree.
He joined them in tears
and looked up with glee,

"Heavenly Father," he said with a smile on his face.
"Thank you for darkness that kept me in place.
For because I waited and trusted in you,
I learned that in prayer
you will always see through."

On the other side
of this forested glen
sat a lone dairy cow
in her shadowy pen.
While the wolf was praying
and calling for light,

she, too, had grown blind
and was lost in the night.

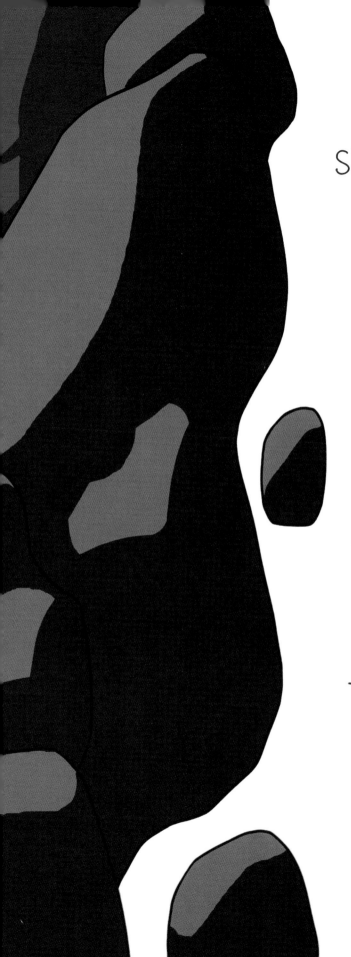

She wandered forward,
from the left
to the right,
and fell in a hole
that was hidden
from sight.

She tried to get out,
but the night
was too thick.
The pit was too deep,
and her fall
was too quick.

So she cried and
she pleaded,
the whole night through,
doing the only thing
that she knew
how to do.

"Heavenly Father,"
she prayed
as the darkness
pulled tight,
"I'm alone and afraid
in this dark,
bitter night."

Then out of the darkness that same light descended, and the fear in her heart began to be mended.
For what she couldn't see in the darkness so deep was the hole she was in really wasn't so steep.

She climbed up some rocks and was soon out onto ground and sent praises to God in a glorious sound.

"Heavenly Father," she said with eyes smiling bright, "I thank you for the darkness that came here tonight.

For had I not prayed when I fell from on high, I wouldn't have learned that you hear when I cry."

Last came the boy, in a simple nightgown,
with his house in the forest, in a small, little town.

He had left his warm bed and the roof with a leak
to get his sick mother water from the creek.

But out
on the way
through his
walk in
the night,
the shadows
fell, and he
was lost
without sight.

A slithery feeling
then moved by his feet
as a snake rustled by
and started to speak.

"You don't need the water,"
the snake's voice
seemed to coo.
"Just stay here with me.
I'll take good care of you."

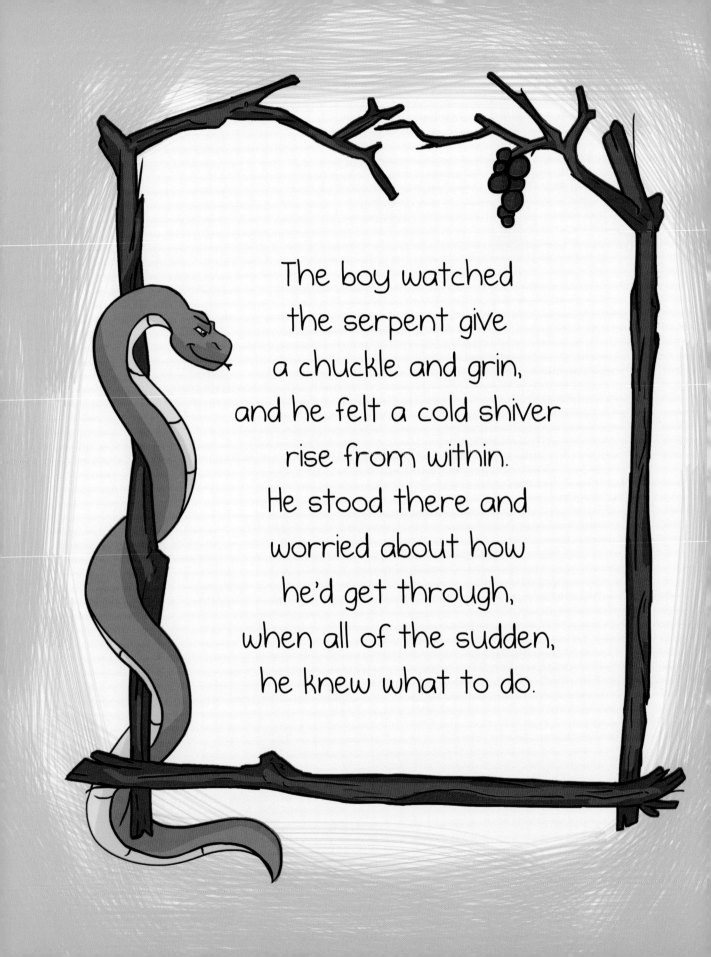

The boy watched
the serpent give
a chuckle and grin,
and he felt a cold shiver
rise from within.
He stood there and
worried about how
he'd get through,
when all of the sudden,
he knew what to do.

With no fear he prayed to his Heavenly Father.
"This snake will not leave, and I need to get water.
My mother is sick, and I can't find my way,
I can't do this without you. Please help me, I pray."

And suddenly lighting the
world all bright
came that same wondrous
flood of radiant light.

The same light that came
when the alpha wolf prayed.
The same light that showed
the cow she was saved.

The snake slinked away,
afraid of the light,
and the boy got his water
and cheered in delight.

"Heavenly Father," he said,
running home to his mom,
"I thank you for darkness,
where cunning snakes roam.
I was scared and alone
and wanted to flee,
but I learned that
you are watching over me.

"I know you will help
me do what is right,
and if I humbly pray,
you will send me your light."

Shadows will come
at the end of each day,
and there may be times
when you lose your way.

But even in darkness
you can feel God's light
as you remember
your prayers in the night.